D1372244

The Grapes of Wrath

John Steinbeck

Abridged and adapted by Tony Napoli

Illustrated by Steve Moore

A PACEMAKER CLASSIC

GLOBE FEARON
EDUCATIONAL PUBLISHER

Supervising Editor: Stephen Feinstein
Project Editor: Karen Bernhaut
Editorial Assistant: Stacie Dozier
Art Director: Nancy Sharkey
Assistant Art Director: Armando Baéz
Production Manager: Penny Gibson
Production Editor: Nicole Cypher
Desktop Specialist: Eric Dawson
Manufacturing Supervisor: Della Smith
Marketing Manager: Marge Curson
Cover Illustration: Steve Moore

Printed in the United States of America
   4 5 6 7 8 9 10 99 98

ISBN 0–835–91072–5

GLOBE FEARON
EDUCATIONAL PUBLISHER

Contents

Cast of Characters

Tom Joad	The son of Ma and Pa Joad; as the story opens, he has just been paroled from prison for killing a man.
Ma Joad	The strong and determined wife and mother who tries to hold the family together
Pa Joad	A tenant farmer who has lost his farm in Oklahoma and moves his family to California
Grampa and Granma	The original settlers on the Joad farm in Oklahoma
Jim Casy	A former preacher who goes with the Joads to California
Rose of Sharon	Tom Joad's pregnant sister
Connie Rivers	Rose of Sharon's husband who eventually leaves the Joad family
Muley Graves	Neighbor of the Joads in Oklahoma who refuses to leave his land
Ivy and Sairy Wilson	Migrants from Kansas who travel with the Joads for awhile
Noah Joad	Tom's older brother
Al Joad	Tom's younger brother, age 16
Ruthie and Winfield Joad	The two youngest Joad children, ages 12 and 10
Mr. and Mrs. Wainwright	The couple who live in the same boxcar as the Joads in the last chapters of the book
Aggie Wainwright	Daughter of the Wainwrights who becomes engaged to Al Joad

1 Going Home

The last rains came gently to the red country and part of the gray country of Oklahoma. In the later part of May the sky grew pale. The clouds that had hung in high puffs for so long were dissolving. The surface of the earth crusted, a thin hard crust.

In the roads where the wheels milled the ground, the dirt crust broke. Then the dust formed. And every moving thing lifted the dust into the air. Men and women huddled in their houses. They tied handkerchiefs over their noses when they went out. And they wore goggles to protect their eyes.

Men stood by their fences and looked at the ruined corn. And the women came out of their houses to stand beside their men—to feel whether this time the men would break. For the corn could go, as long as something else remained.

As the day went forward, the sun became less red. It glared down on the dust-blanketed land. The men sat in the doorways of their houses. Their hands were busy with sticks and little rocks. The men sat still—thinking—figuring.

A huge red transport truck stood in front of the little roadside restaurant. A man walking along the edge of the highway crossed over and walked up to the truck. He put his hand on the front fender and looked at the *No Riders* sticker on the windshield. For a moment he was about to walk on down the road. Instead, he sat on the running board on the side away from the restaurant.

He was not over 30. His eyes were very dark brown. His cheek bones were high and wide, and strong deep lines cut down his cheeks. His hands were hard and shiny with calluses. The man's clothes were new—all of them, cheap and new.

Inside the restaurant the truck driver paid his bill and walked outside. When he got to his truck, the hitchhiker stood up and looked across the windows. "Could ya give me a lift, mister?"

The driver looked quickly back at the restaurant for a second. "Didn't you see the *No Riders* sticker on the windshield?"

"Sure," the man said. "But sometimes a guy will be a good guy even if he carries a sticker."

The driver thought about his answer. He wanted to be a good guy. "Okay, but scrunch down on the running board till we get around the bend," he said. "Don't want others to see."

The hitchhiker did as he was told. It was a mile till the first turn in the road. Then the truck slowed down. The hitchhiker stood up, opened the door, and slipped into the seat. "Thanks, buddy," he said. "I'm pooped out."

"Going far?" the driver asked.

"No! I would have walked if I wasn't so pooped out."

The driver had the tone of a quiet examiner. He seemed to set traps with his questions. "Lookin' for a job?" he asked.

"No, my old man's got a place, 40 acres. He's a cropper, but we've been there a long time."

"A 40-acre cropper, and he hasn't been dusted out, and he hasn't been tractored out?"

"Well, I haven't heard anything lately," the hitchhiker said.

"Been doin' a job?" the driver asked casually.

"Sure have," said the hitchhiker.

"Thought so. I saw your hands. You've been swingin' a pick or an ax. That shines up your hands."

The hitchhiker stared at him. "Like to know anything else? I'll tell you. You don't have to guess."

"Now don't get sore. I wasn't gettin' nosy. I just like to notice things. Makes the time pass."

"I'll tell you anything. Name is Tom Joad. Old man is ol' Tom Joad." His eyes stared at the driver.

They rode for a while talking about this and that. Finally, the driver said, "I train my mind all the time. Suppose I pass a guy on the road. I look at him and later I try to remember everything about him. His clothes, how he walked, how much he weighed. I do it pretty good."

"You sure took a hell of a long time to get to it, buddy," Tom said.

"Get to what? How do you mean?"

Tom's voice became harsh. "You know what I mean. You gave me a going over when I first came in. You know where I come from, don't you?"

"Well, sure. But it ain't none of my business."

"I'm not keeping quiet about it," Tom said. "Sure I been in McAlester. Been there four years." He laughed. "I done time, so what! You want to know what for, don't you?"

"That's none of my affair," the driver said.

Tom pointed up ahead. "I get off there."

The truck stopped at a dirt road that intersected with the highway. Tom got out.

"I'm not a guy to let you down," Tom said. "Homicide. That's a big word—means I killed a guy. Seven years. I got out in four for keepin' my nose clean."

Tom hit the metal door with the palm of his hand. "Thanks for the lift," he said. "So long." He turned and walked down the road.

Tom plodded along the road, dragging his cloud of dust behind him. Ahead he saw a high-domed shell of a land turtle crawling slowly through the dust. When he got to it, he picked it up and rolled it up in his coat.

Up ahead, a scrawny willow tree cast a bit of shade. He needed to get to it, for he was sweating badly now. When he got closer, he saw a man sitting on the ground, leaning against the trunk of the tree.

Tom came up to the tree, and the man looked up at him. Tom said, "Hi. It's hotter than hell on the road."

The man said, "Aren't you young Tom Joad—ol' Tom's boy?"

"Yeah," said Tom. "Going home now."

"You wouldn't remember me, I guess," the man said. "I baptized you."

"Why, you're the preacher," Tom said.

"I was a preacher," the man said seriously. "Reverend Jim Casy. Just Jim Casy now. I haven't got the calling any more.

"I went off and figured some things," Casy said. "I figured about the Holy Spirit and Jesus. I figured, 'Why do we got to hang it on God or Jesus? Maybe it's all men and women we love. Maybe that's the Holy Spirit—the human spirit. Maybe all men got one big soul everybody is a part of. All of a sudden, I knew it. I knew it so deep down that it was true, and I still know it.

"Funny thing," Casy went on. "I was just thinking about ol' Tom Joad when you come along. Thought I'd call on him. How is he?"

"I don't know. I haven't been home in four years."

"Been out traveling around?" Casy asked.

"Didn't you hear about me?" Tom asked. "I was in all the papers."

"No—I never. What?"

Tom told him where he'd been—and why. "I killed a guy in a fight—at a dance. He got a knife in me. I killed him with a shovel that was laying there."

"Then you haven't heard nothing about your folks in four years?" Casy asked.

"Ma sent me a Christmas card two years ago. And last Christmas Granma sent a card. Guess I'll get going," Tom said. "Come along. Pa will be glad to see you."

They walked on. They moved over the curving top of the hill and saw the Joad place below them. And Tom stopped. "It's not the same," he said. "Look at that house. Something's happened. Nobody is there." The two stood and stared at the little cluster of buildings.

2 "There's Nothin' Left"

The owners of the land came onto the land. Or, more often a spokesman for the owners came. Sometimes a bank or finance company owned the land. The owner men sat in the car and explained, you know the land is poor.

The tenant men nodded and drew figures in the dust. Yes, they knew. If the dust only wouldn't fly. If the top would only stay on the soil. Then it might not be so bad.

At last the owner men came to the point. The tenant system won't work any more. One man on a tractor can take the place of 12 or 14 families. Pay him a wage and take all the crop.

The tenant men cried, but it's our land. We measured it and broke it up. We were born on it, we died on it. That's what makes it ours. And if we go, where will we go? How will we go? We got no money.

We're sorry, said the owner men. Maybe you can go on relief. Why don't you go to California? There's work there, and it never gets cold. The owner men started their cars and rolled away.

The Reverend Casy and young Tom stood on a hill and looked down on the Joad place. The small unpainted house was mashed at one corner. The fences were gone. Cotton grew in the dooryard and against the house.

"Geez," Tom said at last. "Maybe they're all dead. But I would have gotten word."

"Maybe they left a letter or something to tell in the house," Casy said. "Let's look."

They walked to the sagging house. The kitchen furniture was all gone. The bedroom was empty, too, except for a woman's broken high button shoe. They went back outside and sat down on the edge of the porch.

"Well, they went—and took everything," Tom said. "There's nothin' left. But something's wrong. I can't put my finger on it."

Just then Tom touched his rolled up coat. "Geez, I forgot the turtle. I was going to give it to little Winfield. But I'm not going to pack it all over the place."

He unwrapped the land turtle and pushed it under the house. But in a moment it was out, headed southwest.

"Somebody is coming," the preacher said. "Look, down there, right through the cotton."

Tom looked where Casy had pointed. "Can't see him for the dust he raises," he said.

Finally, the man got much closer and walked right past the barn. "Why, that's Muley Graves. Hey, Muley! How are you?"

The man stopped, startled by the call. Then he came over quickly. "Well, I'll be—it's Tommy Joad," he said. "When did you get out?"

"Two days ago," Tom said. "Where's my folks, Muley? What's the house all smashed up for, and cotton planted in the dooryard?"

"Well, they were going to stick it out when the bank come. Your grampa stood here with a rifle and blew the headlights off the tractor. But it came just the same and pushed over the house."

"Where's my folks?" Joad spoke angrily.

"They're all at your Uncle John's," Muley said quickly. "Took the stove, bed, everything."

"Oh! Well, what are they doing there?"

"They've been chopping cotton. They're going to get money together so they can buy a car and shove west."

"What happened here?" Casy asked. "Why are they kickin' folks off the land?"

"Dust come up and spoil everything," Muley said. "Man doesn't have enough crop to feed an ant. The folks that own the land say 'we can't afford to keep no tenants.' So, they tractored all the tenants off the land. All except me, and by God I'm not going."

"Well we're not going to walk eight miles to Uncle John's place now," Tom said. "How about if we go to your place, Muley? That's only about a mile."

"Won't do any good," Muley said. "My wife and her brother and the kids all took off and went to California. There wasn't anything to eat. They weren't as mad as me, so they went."

"You should have gone, too," Casy said. "You shouldn't have broken up the family."

"I couldn't," Muley said. "Something just wouldn't let me."

"Well, I'm starving," Tom said. "What have you been doing for food, Muley?"

Muley picked up a sack and emptied it. Two cottontails and a jackrabbit fell out.

Casy picked up one of the cottontails. "You sharin' with us, Muley?" he asked.

They built a fire, ate, and talked for a long time. When it was dark and very late, they saw a glow in the distance. "Somebody saw our fire," Muley said. "Probably the superintendent of this stretch of cotton."

"We're not doing no harm," Tom said.

"Yeah we are," Muley said. "We're trespassing. We can't stay. They've been trying to catch me for two months. Look, if that's a car coming, we go out in the cotton and lay down. Then let 'em try to find us."

The glow got much closer. They quickly put out the fire. The three men ran out into the cotton fields and stretched out.

The car came up to the house and a spotlight came on. The light swung over their heads and crisscrossed the fields. They heard footsteps on the wood. Then the car doors slammed, and the spotlight swept over them again. A moment later, the car started and slipped away.

"If you fellows want to come along, I'll show you where to sleep," Muley said.

"Lead off," said Tom. "We'll follow. I never thought I'd be hiding out on my old man's place."

The three men marched across the fields until they came to a water-cut. They slid down to the bottom of it.

"It's a cave in the bank, isn't it?" Tom asked. "My God, my brother Noah and I dug here when we were kids."

Muley crawled into the cave. Tom settled himself on the clean sand. "I'm not going to sleep in any cave," he said. He rolled his coat under his head. Jim Casy sat down beside him.

"Get some sleep," Tom said. "We'll start for Uncle John's at daybreak."

"I'm not sleeping," Casy said. "I got too much to puzzle with." And with that the preacher threw back his head and gazed at the stars. Tom yawned and brought back one hand under his head.

In the towns, on the edges of towns, in fields, in vacant lots—the Used Car signs were everywhere. Cars lined up, rusty noses forward, tires flat.

Lookin' for a car? There's a car. Run forever. Make it into a truck. Got anything to trade?

Got a pair of mules I'll trade.

Mules! Hey, Joe, hear this? This guy wants to trade mules. Didn't anybody tell you this is the machine age? Well, why not? I'm a sucker.

Muley Graves had awakened Tom when it was still dark. He told Tom he was moving on right then. He refused to go to Uncle John's. He was just going to keep on living like he had been. Later, Tom told the preacher that Muley was getting "as screwy as a gopher."

It was nearly sunrise when Tom and Jim Casy reached Uncle John's place. On the way Tom told the preacher about Uncle John. Years before his young wife was pregnant. One night she got a pain in her stomach. John didn't want to go for a doctor. He told her it was just a stomachache from eating too much.

The next day the young woman was out of her head in pain. She died later that day from a busted appendix. Uncle John blamed himself. After that, he was always giving away stuff to people—especially kids. He still wasn't very happy. But he was a good farmer.

After a while, Tom said, "Look, that's Uncle John's tank."

He walked faster. A strange truck stood in the yard. The front was a sedan, but the top had been cut off in the middle. And the truck bed had been fitted on. Old Tom Joad stood in the bed and was nailing on the top rails of the truck sides.

Tom sidled up to the truck and leaned against it. Tom looked up at the aging, graying man on the truck. He wet his lips and said softly, "Pa."

"What do you want?" old Tom mumbled around a mouthful of nails. He looked over the side of the truck. He seemed angry at being interrupted. Then his eyes looked at Tom's face. "It's Tommy," he said. "It's Tommy come home. You ain't busted out? You ain't got to hide?"

"Naw," Tom said. "I'm paroled. I'm free."

Old Tom dropped down from the truck. "We're going to California," he said. "We were going to write and tell you. But you're back," he said almost in disbelief. "You can go with us!" A noise came from inside the house. "Let's surprise 'em," Old Tom said.

Tom said, "You remember the preacher, Pa. I met him on the road."

Pa shook hands. "You're welcome here."

"Glad to be here," Casy said.

They went into the house. Pa said, "Ma, there are a couple of fellows just come up the road. They wonder if we could spare a bite."

Tom heard his mother's calm, friendly voice. "Let them come," she said. "We got plenty." Tom stood outside the door, a dark figure outlined by the bright sunshine. His mother couldn't tell who it was. "Come in," she said. When Tom stepped over the doorsill, Ma's eyes opened wide. "Thank God!" she said. Suddenly her face was worried. "Tommy, you ain't wanted? You didn't bust loose?"

"No, Ma. Parole. I got the papers here." He touched his chest.

His mother moved toward him. She felt his arm, the soundness of his muscles. Her fingers went up to his cheek as a blind man's fingers might. And her joy was nearly like sorrow.

After a while, Tom spoke again. "Ma, when I saw what they done to our house—"

"Tommy, don't you go fighting them alone," she said passionately. "They'll hunt you down like a coyote. I've been thinking, wondering. They say there's a hundred thousand of us

shoved out. If we were all mad the same way, they wouldn't hunt anybody down."

"Many folks feel that way?" he demanded.

"I don't know. They're just kind of stunned. They walk around like they were half asleep."

"Ma, you were never like this before."

Her face hardened and her eyes grew cold. "I never had my house pushed over," she said. "I never had my family stuck out on the road. I never had to sell—everything."

Soon, Granma, Grampa, and Tom's older brother Noah came in from the barn. They were thrilled to see that Tom had come home. Tom asked about the rest of the family.

"Uncle John's gone to Sallisaw with a load of stuff to sell," Pa said. "Ruthie and Winfield went with him. Rose of Sharon is with Connie's folks. By God! You didn't even know Rose of Sharon is married to Connie Rivers. She's pregnant."

"Geez," Tom said. "Rose of Sharon was just a little kid. Now she's going to have a baby. So much happens in four years." He paused. "When do you figure to start out west?"

"Well, as soon as we sell the rest of this stuff," Pa said. "Maybe tomorrow or the day after. We only got about $200. We sold all the stuff at our place. And the whole bunch of us chopped cotton—even Grampa."

Just then, Tom's younger brother Al came into the house. He'd spent the last few days saying good-bye to his friends.

"Hello, Al," Tom said. "Geez, you're growing like a bean. I wouldn't have known you."

Al shook hands warmly. For the past four years he had been admired by boys his own age because his brother Tom had killed a man.

"Did—did you bust out of jail?" he asked.

"No," said Tom. "I got paroled."

"Oh." Al sounded a little disappointed.

3 Heading West

In the little houses the tenant people went through their belongings and the belongings of their fathers and grandfathers. They picked over their possessions for the journey west.

Harness, carts, seeders, little bundles of hoes. Bring them out. Pile them up. Load them in the wagon. Take them to town. Sell them for what you can get. Sell the team and the wagon, too. No more use for anything.

Well, take it—all junk—and give me five dollars. You're not buying only junk, you're buying junked lives. What's more, you're buying bitterness. Buying a plow to plow your own children under. We could have saved you, but you cut us down. And soon you will be cut down, and there will be none of us to save you.

And the tenant men came walking back. They walked back to their farms, hands in their pockets, hats pulled down, shoes kicking the red dust up. Maybe we can start again, in the new rich land— in California, where the fruit grows. We'll start over.

Got to get out quick now. We can't wait. And they piled up the goods in the yards and set fire to them. Then they loaded up the cars and drove away in the dust.

The truck was loaded with every last moveable thing. Then Al drove it into Sallisaw to sell everything. Tom walked into the kitchen where Ma was washing the children's clothes in a bucket.

"I like to think how nice it's going to be, maybe, in California," Ma said. "Never cold. And fruit every place. Little white houses in among the orange trees. I wonder—if we all get jobs and work—maybe we can get one of those little white houses."

Tom watched her working and his eyes smiled. "It's done you good just thinking about it," he said. "I knew a fellow from California at McAlester. He said there's too many folks looking for work there right now. And he said that the folks that pick the fruit live in dirty old camps and don't hardly get enough to eat. He said wages are low and hard to get."

A shadow crossed her face. "Oh, that's not so," she said. "Your father got a handbill telling how they need folks to work. It costs them good money to get them handbills out. Why would they spend that money just to lie?"

"I don't know, Ma. Maybe—" He looked out at the hot sun, shining on the red earth.

"Maybe what?"

"Maybe it's nice, like you said."

Ma walked out of the house, her arms loaded down with the wet clothes. Tom followed her outside and sat on the doorstep. "Here comes the preacher, walking around from the back side of the barn," he said.

Casy walked up to them. "I got to get going west," he said suddenly. "I wonder if I can go along with you folks." He stood there, a little embarrassed by his speech.

Ma looked to Tom to speak, because he was a man. When he didn't, she said, "Why we'd be proud to have you. I can't say right now. Pa says all the men will talk tonight and figure when we'll start. And if there's room, I'm pretty sure you can come."

The preacher sighed. "I'll go anyway," he said. "I can't stay here anymore. I got to go where the folks are going. I'll work in the fields and maybe I'll be happy."

"You're not going to preach?" Tom asked.

"I'm not gonna preach," Casy said. "I'm gonna work in the fields, and I'm gonna be near the folks. I'm not gonna try to teach them anything. I'm gonna try to learn."

In the late afternoon, the truck came back, bumping and rattling in the dust. Al sat bent over the wheel in the driver's seat. Pa and Uncle

John sat next to him. Standing in the truck bed, holding onto the bars of the sides, rode the others.

There was 12-year-old Ruthie and 10-year-old Winfield. They were grimy-faced and wild, their eyes tired but excited. Beside them stood Rose of Sharon, pregnant and careful. She balanced on her toes now, for her baby's sake. Her round soft face already showed signs of her soon to be motherhood. Connie, her 19-year-old husband, was next to her. He was a sharp-faced young man with pale blue eyes. He was a hard worker and would make a good husband.

They were all tired on the truck. And the men up front were angry. They had only gotten $18 for every moveable thing on the farm: the horses, the wagon, the tools, and all the furniture from the house.

The young children greeted Tom with great excitement. Rose of Sharon introduced Tom to her husband. She told Tom her baby wasn't due until the winter. Tom laughed and said, "Gonna get him born in an orange ranch, huh?"

That night the family council met. Pa said the family had a total of $154. But they still needed to buy better tires for the truck. Then Tom brought up the matter of taking the preacher along.

Pa was worried that they already had too many mouths to feed, and the truck would be overloaded. But Ma said there never was a Joad that refused food, or shelter, or a lift on the road to anyone. She said that there wasn't enough room for everyone now. One more wasn't going to make much difference.

After Ma spoke, no one objected to the preacher coming along. Tom called Casy in. He even invited him to sit in on the meeting and help make the final decisions.

The one big decision they had to make was when to leave. All that was left to do was to slaughter two pigs, salt the meat, and load the truck with the few belongings they could take. They decided to begin right after the meeting. They'd all pitch in, work through the night, and leave at first daylight.

Out in the dark yard, Pa and Al loaded the truck, working by lantern light. At the bottom, they put tools, boxes of clothes, kitchen utensils, and pots, pans, and dishes. Then over the top they laid the mattresses.

Just before dawn, Muley Graves appeared, almost out of nowhere. Pa offered him some food. But he refused.

"I was just walking around," he said. "I thought you'd be going, and I'd say good-bye."

"You want to squeeze in with us?" Pa asked. "We'd try to make room for you."

"Sometimes I think I might," he said. "But I won't."

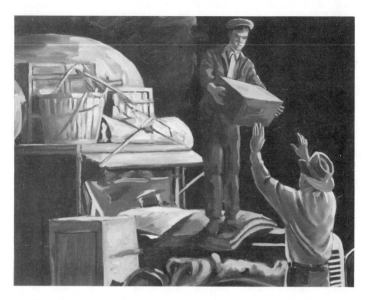

"You're going to die out in the field some day, Muley," Noah said.

"I know, I thought about that," Muley said. "It don't make a difference. What I really came to say—if you come across my folks in California, tell them I'm well. Don't let on I'm livin' this way. Tell them I'll come out as soon as I get the money."

"Will you?" Ma asked.

"No," Muley said. "I'm not ever going."

In a little while, they were all ready. When everyone was on top of the truck, Pa called to the dogs. But only one came.

"Got to leave the other two," Pa said. "Muley, will you look after them?"

"Yeah," he said. "I'd like to have a couple of dogs."

"Take them chickens, too," Pa said.

Al got in behind the wheel. "So long, Muley," he said.

The truck crawled up the little hill, and the red dust rose up around them. The people on the top looked back. They saw Muley standing forlornly in the dooryard looking after them. The cotton fields lined the road. And the truck crawled slowly through the dust toward the highway and the west.

4 Sharing the Load

Highway 66 is the main migrant road. 66—the long concrete path across the country, from the Mississippi to Bakersfield. It runs over the red lands and the gray lands, twisting up into the mountains, then crossing the Divide. Then it runs down into the bright and terrible desert to the mountains again, and into the rich California valleys.

The people in flight streamed out on 66, sometimes a single car, sometimes a little caravan. All day they rolled slowly along the road, and at night they stopped near water. The men driving the trucks and the overloaded cars listened in fear. How far between towns? It is a terror between towns. If something breaks we camp right here while Jim walks to town and gets a part and walks back. And how much food we got?

People in flight along 66. Two hundred and fifty thousand people over the road. Fifty thousand old cars—wounded, steaming. Wrecks along the road, abandoned. Well, what happened to the folks in that car? Did they walk? Where does the courage come from? Where does the terrible faith come from?

The old, overloaded Hudson creaked and grunted to the highway at Sallisaw and turned west. The sun was blinding. Al was behind the wheel. His face was set, his whole body listening to the car. Granma was beside him on the seat, half asleep. Ma sat next to her, one elbow out the window, her skin reddening under the fierce sun.

After several hours, they stopped at a service station. They needed gas and water. Somehow they had forgotten the gallon jug.

"You folks aim to buy anything? Gasoline or stuff," the station man said.

"Need some gas, mister," Al said.

"Got any money?"

"Sure. Think we're begging?"

"Well, that's all right, folks," the man said quickly. "Help yourself to water." Then he quickly explained. "Road is full of people, come in to use water, dirty up the toilet, and don't buy a thing. Got no money. Come begging for a gallon of gasoline to move on. I don't know what the country's coming to," the man continued. "Loads of folks go by every day. Folks all movin' west. Where are they goin'? What are they going to do?"

"Doin' the same as us," Tom said angrily. "Goin' someplace to live. Tryin' to get along."

"Well, I don't know what the country's comin' to," the man repeated.

When everybody had gotten a drink and gone to the bathroom, they were ready to start again. Tom came up beside Al. "You want I should drive for a piece?" Tom asked.

"I'm not tired," Al said.

"Well, you didn't get any sleep last night. I took a snooze this morning. Get up on top. I'll take over."

"All right," Al said reluctantly. "But watch the oil gauge. And take it pretty slow, Tom. It's overloaded."

Tom laughed. "I'll watch it. You can rest easy."

Tom drove slowly and carefully in the traffic. And then they were out on 66—the great western road. The sun was sinking and the windshield was bright with dust.

Ma had been silent for a long time. "Maybe we better find a place to stop before sunset," she said at last. "I got to get some pork boiling and some bread made. That takes time."

"Sure," Tom agreed. "We're not going to make this trip in one jump. Might as well stretch ourselves."

"Tom," Ma went on. "Your pa told me about you crossing the state line—"

"Yeah? What about it, Ma?" Tom said.

"Well I'm scared about it," she said. "It will make you kind of running away. Maybe they'll catch you."

"Don't you worry," he said. "There are lots of fellows out on parole, and they're more goin' west all the time. If I get caught for anything else out west, then they'll send me back. But if I don't do no crimes, they won't give a darn."

"Well, I'm scared," she said. "The minute you cross the state line, you done a crime."

"Well, that's better than sticking around Sallisaw and starving to death," he said. "We better look for a place to stop."

They drove until they came to a ditch where a drain pipe went under the road. An old touring car was pulled off the highway and a little tent was beside it. The hood of the car was up. A middle aged man stood looking down at the motor.

Tom pulled along side. He asked the man if it was legal to stop there for the night. The man said he'd only stopped because his car broke down. Tom said, "Well, you got a right to say if you want neighbors or not."

"Why sure, come on off the road," the man said. He called to his wife. "Sairy, there are some folks going to stay with us. Come out and say hello. Sairy ain't well."

A small, shuddering woman came out of the tent. She held herself upright by a tent flap. The hand holding onto the canvas was a skeleton covered with wrinkled skin. "Tell 'em welcome," she said. "Good and welcome."

Tom drove the truck into the field beside the touring car. And the two families got acquainted.

"Wilson, Ivy Wilson," the man said. "From Galena, Kansas."

"We're Joads," said Pa. "We come from right near Sallisaw, Oklahoma."

Noah, Uncle John, and Casy began to unload the truck. They helped Grampa down. He sat down on the ground, limply, and stared ahead. "Are you sick, Grampa?" Noah asked.

"Darn right," Grampa said. "I'm sicker than hell." And without warning, he began to cry. His old lips tightened over his mouth, and he sobbed hoarsely. Ma rushed over to him and helped him into the tent.

Grampa seemed to be struggling. All his muscles twitched. He suddenly jarred as though under a heavy blow. He lay still and his breath was stopped. Casy looked down at the old man's face. It was turning a blackish purple.

Granma began to scream at Casy. "Pray," she said. "Pray, pray, I tell you," she yelled.

Casy began to pray. Grampa's breathing became louder and more uneven. Finally, a long gasping sigh came from the open mouth. And then there was a crying release of air. Casy looked down into Grampa's eyes. They were

clear and deep, and there was a peaceful look in them.

Sairy Wilson took Granma outside. The old woman was calm and walked with dignity. Casy pushed back the tent flap and stepped outside.

Pa asked softly, "What was it?"

"Stroke," Casy said. "A quick stroke."

The family became a unit. Everyone knew it would cost quite a bit of money to have someone take Grampa to a town and bury him there. So, it was decided to bury him by the side of the road. They knew they'd be breaking the law. But they also knew they might not have enough money to make it to California any other way.

Ma and Sairy Wilson laid Grampa out in a quilt. Tom wrote a note on a page from a Bible. The note said who was buried in the grave and the fact that Grampa had died of natural causes. Then he put the note in a bottle beside the body.

Pa and the other men took turns digging the grave. When they finished, Casy said a few words over the body. Then Grampa was laid to rest.

Later that night the Joads and the Wilsons came to a decision. They would travel together to California. Al and Tom would fix the Wilson's car, and try to keep it from breaking down every few miles. Meanwhile, some of the Joad family members could ride in the car. That would relieve the overloaded truck. They could make better traveling time, and get up the hills easier.

The Wilsons were worried about being a burden. "If I get sick again, you got to go on and get there," Sairy Wilson said.

"We're gonna see you get through," Ma said.

Both families moved lazily to their sleep. The fire died down, and the stars descended. Soon, the families were quiet and sleeping. Only Sairy Wilson was awake. She stared into the sky and braced her body firmly against the pain.

5 Keeping the Family Together

The western land, nervous under the beginning change. The great owners, nervous, sense a change. The great owners strike at the widening government and the growing labor unity. Not knowing these are results, not causes. The causes lie deep and simple. The causes are a hunger in the stomach, multiplied a million times. And a hunger in a single soul, hunger for joy and some security, multiplied a million times.

One man, one family driven from the land. I lost my land, a single tractor took my land. I am alone, and I am bewildered. And in the night one family camps in a ditch. Then another family pulls in and the tents come out.

The two men squat and talk as the women and children listen. "I lost my land" becomes "We lost our land." The danger is here, for two men are not as lonely and confused as one.

If you who own the things people must have could understand this, you might save yourself. If you could separate causes from results, you might survive. But you cannot.

Along 66 the hamburger stands: Al and Susy's Place, Carl's Lunch, Will's Eats. Two gasoline pumps in front, a screen door, a long bar, and a foot rail.

Minnie or Susy or Mae is behind the counter. They take orders in a soft, low voice. But they call them out to the cook with a screech like a peacock. The cook is Joe or Carl or Al, sweaty in a white apron.

The truck drivers are the backbone of the joint. Where the trucks stop, that's where the customers come. Mae really smiles with all her might at truck drivers.

An old sedan pulls off the highway. It's piled to the top with stuff, and on the very top two boys ride. A dark-haired man walks into the diner followed by the two boys. The boys are dressed in ragged, patched overalls and nothing else.

The man said, "Could you see your way to sell us a loaf of bread, ma'am?"

"This isn't a grocery store," Mae said. "We got bread to make sandwiches. Why don't you buy a sandwich?"

"We can't," the man said. "We got to make a dime do all of us."

Mae said, "You can't get a loaf of bread for a dime. We only got fifteen-cent loaves."

From behind her Al growled, "God Almighty, Mae. Give 'em bread."

Mae shrugged her shoulders. She took out a loaf from a drawer. "This is a fifteen-cent loaf."

"Can't you see your way clear to cut off ten cents' worth?" the man asked.

"Mae, give them the loaf," Al snarled.

"No, we want to buy ten cents' worth of it," the man said. "We don't want to rob you."

"Go ahead, Al says to take it," Mae said and shoved the bread across the counter.

The man reached into a leather pouch and found a dime. When he put it on the counter, he had a penny with it. He was about to put the penny back into the pouch, when his eyes fell on the boys. They were frozen before the candy counter.

The man pointed to the big long sticks of peppermint. "Are those penny candies, ma'am?"

The little boys raised their eyes to Mae's face and held their breath.

"Oh—them. Well, no—they're two for a penny," she said.

"Well, give me two," the man said. The boys expelled their breath softly. Mae held the big sticks out. "Take them," the man said.

The boys took the sticks and held them down at their sides. The man said thanks, picked up the bread, and went out the door. The boys leaped like chipmunks on top of the load. The man started his car, and the sedan climbed up the highway and continued west. From inside, Mae and two truck drivers stared after them.

"Those weren't two for a penny candy," Big Bill said. "They were a nickel a piece."

"What's that to you?" Mae said fiercely.

"We have to get goin'," the other driver said.

They reached into their pockets. Bill put a coin on the counter. The other man looked at it and matched it. They marched to the door.

"So long," said Bill.

Mae called. "Hey! Wait a minute. You got change." The screen door slammed.

Mae looked at the two half-dollars on the counter. Coffee and a piece of pie was 15 cents.

The Joads and Wilsons crawled westward as a unit. Through western Oklahoma and across the Panhandle of Texas they went. Little by little they settled into the new way of life. The land rolled out before them. First the end of Texas, then New Mexico, and in the far distance, the mountains stood. They crawled to the Pecos River and crossed at Santa Rosa. And then they went on for 20 miles.

Al drove the car, and his mother sat beside him. Rose of Sharon sat beside Ma. Ahead the truck crawled, with Tom at the wheel. The hot air folded in waves over the land, and the mountains shivered in the heat.

Al grew tense over the wheel. A little rattle had developed in the engine. He speeded up, and the rattle increased. Then it increased to a metallic pounding. Al blew his horn and pulled the car to the side of the road. Ahead the truck pulled up and then backed slowly.

Tom got out and came over. "What's the matter, Al?" he asked.

"Listen," Al said. He speeded the motor. The rattling sound was louder now. "Con-rod bearing, isn't it?" Al said.

"Sounds like it," Tom said. "I'll pull ahead and find a flat place to stop. You come ahead slow. Don't knock the pan out of it."

"I don't know what made it go out," Al said. "I gave it plenty of oil."

"It's not your fault," Ma said. "You did everything right. Is it real bad?"

"Well, it's hard to get at," Al answered. "And we got to get a new one. I'm sure glad Tom's here. I've never fixed a bearing."

The families gathered around the touring car. Tom said it would take a good two or three days to go to the nearest town, find the part, and then put it in. Pa was afraid they would start to run out of money. Mr. Wilson wanted the Joads to continue on without them. Pa refused.

Tom said he had an idea. He and Casy would stay behind and get the car fixed. Everyone else would pile into the truck and keep going. The sooner they all got to California, the sooner they'd make some money.

Pa, Uncle John, Al, Casy, and the Wilsons all agreed that it sounded like a sensible idea. "Well, if that's the way it's going to be, we better move along," Pa said. "Maybe we can squeeze in 100 miles before we stop."

Ma stepped in front of him. "I'm not going to go," she said.

"What do you mean, you're not gonna go? You got to go. You got to look after the family." Pa was amazed at the revolt.

Ma stepped back to the touring car and reached for the floor of the back seat. She pulled out a jack handle and balanced it in her hand. "I'm not gonna go," she said.

Pa looked helplessly about the group. "She's sassy," he said. "I've never seen her so sassy." Ruthie giggled.

"Ma, what's eating you?" Tom said.

"You've done this without thinkin' much," Ma said. "What do we got left in the world? Nothin' but us. Nothin' but the folks. We come out, and we lost Grampa right away. Now, you want to bust up the folks—"

"Ma, we're going to catch up with you."

"Suppose we camped and you went on by," she said. "Suppose we go on through, how do we

know where to leave word. We got a bitter road ahead. Granma's sick up on the truck, gettin' like Grampa. We got a long, bitter road ahead.

"The money we'd make wouldn't do no good," Ma went on. "I can't say anything if the Wilsons here and the preacher want to go. But I'm going wild with this here jack handle if my own folks bust up."

"Ma we can't all camp here," Tom said softly. "There's no shade or water."

"All right," Ma said. "We'll go along and stop the first place there's water and shade. Then the truck will come back and take you to town and bring you back."

Tom turned to his father. "Pa," he said, "if you were to rush her on one side and me on the other, and the rest pile on, maybe we can get Ma without more than two or three of us gettin' killed. But, if you're not willin' to get your head smashed, I guess Ma gets her way." He turned back to his mother. "You win, Ma. Put away that jack handle before you hurt somebody."

Tom and Casy stayed behind and worked on the car. Al took the truck with the others on down the road. He was gone for quite a while. By the time he'd returned, Tom had removed the oil pan and the broken part.

"Where did you take the folks?" Tom asked.

"We came to a camp," Al said. "Costs 50 cents a day to stay there."

Tom looked at the lowering sun. "Casy, somebody's got to stay with the car, or it'll get stripped. Will you?"

"Sure, I'll stay," Casy said.

Tom got in beside Al. "We'll get back as soon as we can. But we can't tell how long."

"I'll be here," Casy said.

The truck moved off in the late afternoon. "He's a nice fellow," Tom said. "He thinks about stuff all the time."

"Well, heck—if you've been a preacher, I guess you got to," Al said.

Al and Tom got lucky. They found a wrecking yard not too far away. They got a matching con-rod, and it only cost them a dollar. They also bought a small socket wrench and a flashlight for another 60 cents.

Casy was surprised to see them back so soon. The three men worked through the evening to repair the car. When they were done, they started the car and listened to it idle. It sounded fine.

"You make a darn good mechanic," Al said to Tom. "What are we going to do now, go on to the camp?"

"I don't know," Tom said. "Maybe they'd charge us an extra half-buck. Let's go on and talk to the folks—tell them we're fixed. Then maybe we'll move on."

When they arrived at the camp, the proprietor wanted to charge them another 50 cents. Tom was angry. He almost started a fight. But Pa said not to make trouble.

Tom spoke briefly with Ma. He told her the car was fixed, and they'd be ready to start again in the morning. He said he'd take the car and spend the night a little ways up the road. Al would stay with the family, and Uncle John would go with Tom and Casy.

The three men went out the gate and climbed into the Dodge. Tom started the car and pulled onto the road. The road spread dimly under the weak lights of the car.

6 Across the Great Desert

The cars of the migrant people moved out onto the great cross-country highway. In the daylight they scuttled like bugs westward. And as the dark caught them, they gathered like bugs near shelter and water.

These people were lonely and confused. They had all come from a place of sadness and worry and defeat. And they were all going to a new mysterious place. Because of all this, they huddled together. They shared their lives, their food, and the things they hoped for in the new country.

So, it might be that one family camped near a spring. And another camped for the spring and for company. Then a third camped because two families had pioneered the place and found it good. And when the sun went down, perhaps 20 families and 20 cars were there.

In the evening a strange thing happened. The 20 families became one family. The children were the children of all. The loss of home became one loss. And the golden time in the West became one dream.

The Joad family moved slowly westward up into the mountains of New Mexico. They climbed into the high country of Arizona. Through a gap they looked down on the Painted Desert.

They drove all day and came to the mountains in the night. When daylight came, they saw the Colorado River below them.

"We're there! We're in California!" Pa called.

Tom said. "We got to get to the water and rest."

The Joads and Wilsons drove to the river and stopped. There was a little encampment by the river, 11 tents near the water, and swamp grass on the ground.

The families pitched their tents. Then while the children played, the older men went down to the river to bathe.

"Like to just stay here," Noah said lazily. "Like to lay here forever. Never get hungry and never get sad."

Two men dressed in jeans and sweaty blue shirts came up to them. "Mind if we come in?" one man said.

"It's not our river," Tom said. "We'll lend you a piece of it."

"Goin' west?" Pa asked the men politely.

"Nope. We come from there. Goin' back home. We can't make a livin' out there."

"Where's home?" Tom asked.

"Panhandle, come from near Pampa."

"Can you make a livin' there?" Pa asked.

"Nope. But at least we can starve to death with folks we know. Won't have a bunch of fellows that hate us to starve with."

"What makes them hate you?" Pa asked.

"I don't know," the man said. "But don't take my word. Go see for yourself."

"Yeah, but a fellow likes to know what he's getting into," Tom said.

"You get across the desert and come into country around Bakersfield," the man said. "You never saw such pretty country. You'll pass land that's flat and fine. You can't have none of that land. That's the Land and Cattle Company. If they don't want to work it, it's not going to get worked."

"Good land, and they're not workin' it?" Pa said.

"That will get you a little mad. But that's nothing. People are going to have a look in their eye that says, 'I don't like you.' They'll be deputy sheriffs and they'll push you around.

"They hate you because they're scared," the man went on. "They know a hungry fellow is going to get food even if he's got to take it. You've never been called an Okie yet?"

"What's an Okie?" Tom asked.

"Well, it used to mean you were from Oklahoma. Now it means you're a dirty bum."

"Suppose a fellow worked and saved. Could he get a little land?"

The man laughed. "You're not going to get any steady work. Going to scramble for your dinner every day."

"Isn't there anything nice out there at all?" Pa asked.

"Sure, nice to look at. But you can't have none of it." The man stood up and faced him. "Look mister, I don't know everything. You might go out there and fall into a steady job. And I'd be a liar. Then you might never get work, and I warned you. I can tell you most of the folks are pretty miserable."

Pa turned his head and looked at Uncle John. "You never was a fellow to say much," Pa said. "But I'll be darned if you opened your mouth twice since we left home. What do you think about this here?"

Uncle John scowled. "I don't think nothin' about it," he said. "None of this talk is going to keep us from going there. When we get there, we get there. When we get a job, we'll work. And when we don't, we'll sit on our tail. This talk isn't going to do any good."

"Uncle John talks sense," Tom said. "We going on tonight, Pa?"

"Might as well," Pa said.

"Then I'm going to go into the brush and get some sleep." Tom stood up and waded to the shore. He walked in among the willows and crawled into a cave. And Noah followed him.

"Tom! I'm not going on," Noah said.

"What do you mean?"

"I'm not going to leave this river."

"You're crazy," Tom said.

"Get myself a piece of line. I'll catch fish. Fellow can't starve beside a nice river."

"How about the family? How about Ma?"

"You know how it is, Tom. You know the folks are nice to me. But they don't really care for me."

"You're crazy," Tom said.

"You tell Ma, Tom."

"Now look here," Tom began.

"No, it's no use," Noah said. "I can't leave this here river. You tell Ma." He walked away.

Tom started to follow. Then he stopped. He saw Noah disappear into the brush, then appear again. He followed the edge of the river until he disappeared into the willows. Tom walked back to his cave and lay down to sleep.

When Tom walked back to the camp, he found Ma right away. He told her about Noah. She was silent for a long time. Then she said, "Family's falling apart. I just don't know."

"He'll be all right, Ma," Tom said. "He's a funny kind of fellow."

Ma told Tom that a lawman had come by. He was nasty and told her they'd better not be there by the morning. Ma said she was so angry she almost hit the man with a skillet. Soon the rest of the men came up from where they'd been sleeping by the willows. They all decided it was best to move on now and cross the desert.

Mr. Wilson came over and said they couldn't go on. His wife was too ill to travel. He insisted the Joads move on without them. He asked Casy to visit his wife before they left.

When the preacher went in the Wilson tent, Sairy asked him to pray. She knew she was dying. Casy didn't want to. But, finally he agreed to say a silent one. When he was finished, she said, "That's what I needed. Somebody close enough to pray."

The Joads loaded up the truck again. Pa offered Mr. Wilson some potatoes, pork, and a few dollars. But Mr. Wilson refused. Ma put the food and the money on the ground anyway. "If you don't get them, somebody else will," she said.

Mr. Wilson turned around and walked back into his tent. The family climbed into the truck. "Good-bye Mr. and Mrs. Wilson," Pa called.

There was no answer from the tent. The truck crawled up the rough road toward the highway. Ma looked back. Wilson stood in front of his tent, staring after them. His hat was in his hand.

The hours passed. On the back of the truck Ma lay on the mattress beside Granma. Ma could feel the struggling body and the struggling heart. And Ma said over and over, "All right. It's going to be all right. You know the family has got to get across. You know that."

It was almost midnight when they neared Daggett where the inspection station was. They stopped and the guard wanted to search all their stuff. Tom asked why. "Agricultural inspection," the guard said.

Ma got down. "We got a sick old lady," she said. "We got to get her to a doctor. We can't wait. I swear we haven't got anything."

The guard insisted. Then he shot a flashlight beam on Granma. "By God, she is," he said. "Go ahead. You can get a doctor in Barstow, about eight miles ahead."

They drove on. When they reached Barstow, Tom stopped. But when he talked to Ma, she said, "It's all right. I don't want to stop here because I'm afraid we won't get across."

"But how's Granma?" Tom said.

"She's all right, drive on," Ma insisted.

All night they bore on through the hot darkness. Finally, the dawn showed high

mountains in the west. They drove through Tehachapi in the morning glow, and the sun came up behind them. Suddenly, they saw the great valley below them.

Tom slammed on the brakes. "Look!" he said. The vineyards, the orchards, the great flat valley was green and beautiful. The trees and the farm houses were set in rows.

"God Almighty," Pa said.

The family got down to look. When Ma walked over, she looked terrible. "My God, Ma, are you sick?" Tom asked.

"You say we're across?" she asked.

"Look!" Tom exclaimed.

"Thank God," she said. "The family's here."

"You sick?"

"No, just tired," Ma said.

"Was Granma bad?"

Ma raised her eyes and looked over the valley. "Granma's dead."

"When?" Pa asked.

"Before they stopped us last night."

"That's why you didn't want them to look."

"I was afraid we wouldn't get across."

She put up her hands and covered her face. "Now she can get buried in a nice green place."

The family looked at Ma with a little terror at her strength. They climbed back on the truck and continued on. They moved to their places and tried to keep their eyes from the covered figure.

They drove down the mountain. "I guess we got to go to the coroner, wherever he is," Tom said. "We got to get her buried decent. How much money we got left, Pa?"

"About $40."

Tom laughed. "Geez, we sure aren't bringing anything with us."

And the truck rolled down the mountain into the great valley.

7 Getting Pushed Around

Once California belonged to Mexico and its land to Mexicans. Then a horde of feverish Americans poured in. And such was their hunger for land that they stole it. They put up houses and barns. And they turned the earth and planted crops.

The Mexicans could not resist. They wanted nothing in the world as desperately as the Americans wanted land.

Generations passed. Now farming became an industry. And the owners imported slaves, although they did not call them slaves. They were Chinese, Japanese, Mexicans, Filipinos. And the farms grew larger and the owners fewer.

Then the owners no longer worked on their farms. They farmed on paper. They forgot the land, the smell, the feel of it. They remembered only that they owned it.

Then the dispossessed were drawn west—from Kansas, Oklahoma, Texas, New Mexico. Families dusted out, tractored out. Carloads, caravans, homeless and hungry. They had hoped to find a home. But they only found hatred.

The homeless drove into towns. They scoured the farms for work. Where can we sleep tonight?

Well, there is a Hooverville on the edge of the river. There's a whole raft of Okies there. They drove there. And they never asked again, for there was a Hooverville on the edge of every town.

Everywhere people starving. Kids starving and crying in their sleep. Our people are good people. Our people are kind people. Pray God some day kind people won't all be poor. Pray God some day a kid can eat.

Pa sighed deeply. "There was nothin' else to do," he said.

"I know," Ma said. "She would have liked a nice funeral, though. She always wanted one."

The family had just come from the coroner's office in Bakersfield. They answered questions and waited while the body was examined for cause of death. Then they left the body to be buried by the county.

"We didn't have enough," Pa said. "A coffin, embalming, a preacher would have cost ten times what we got."

"I know," Ma said. "I got to get it out of my head." Her jaw tightened. "We got to get going and find a place to stay."

They drove out of town. By a bridge they found a collection of tents and shacks. There was no order to the camp. The shacks were made of boards and tattered canvas. Some of the tents were weathered, but neatly set up. Others were ragged, torn in strips, and mended with pieces of wire.

There were boxes, mattresses, and clothes lines everywhere. Far down the line, a few children stood and stared at the newly arrived truck. The little boys moved toward it. They were in overalls and bare feet, their hair gray with dust.

A young man was working on an old Buick in front of a tent. When he saw the Joad truck, he wandered over. Pa asked him if they could camp there.

"Sure. Why not?" the man said. "You folks just come across?"

"Yeah," said Tom.

"Never been in a Hooverville before?"

"Where's Hooverville?"

"This is it," the man said.

"Oh," Tom said.

"Let's get the camp up," Ma said. "I'm tuckered out. Maybe we can all rest."

While the men set up camp, Tom asked the young man about work.

"There's no crop right now," the man said. "We're moving on, as soon as I get my car fixed. We heard there was work up north, around Salinas."

"Back home some fellows come through with handbills. Says they need lots of people out here to work the crops."

The man laughed. "They say there's 300 thousand of us folks here. And I bet every one of them has seen those handbills."

"If they don't need folks, why do they put out those handbills?" Tom asked.

"Because when there's a hundred men who want one job, you can offer them a nickel. And they'll kill each other for that nickel. Know what I made on the last job I had? Fifteen cents an hour. Ten hours for a dollar and a half, and you can't stay on the place. You got to burn gasoline gettin' there."

The man was panting with anger, and his eyes blazed with hate. "That's why them handbills were out. You can print a hell of a lot of handbills with what you save payin' 15 cents an hour."

Tom walked down past the Joad tent. Ma was making a meat stew. Several of the children in the camp had gathered around the pot. All of them looked self-consciously at their feet.

Tom walked around the side of the tent. He found Casy sitting on the earth, wisely regarding one bare foot. Tom sat down beside him.

"I've been thinking," Casy said. "There's an army of us without a harness. Every place we've stopped, folks are hungry. And when they eat, they're still not fed.

"I'm not doing anybody any good," Casy went on. "Me or anybody else. I was thinkin' I'd go off by myself. I'm eatin' your food and takin' up room. And I'm not givin' you nothing. Maybe I could get a steady job and pay back the stuff you've given me."

"Don't go away yet," Tom said. "Stick around until tomorrow. Tomorrow we'll go out and look for work."

A little later, Al showed up with the young man Tom had spoken with earlier. His name was Floyd. He told Tom he heard there was work up north, about 200 miles away. Al wanted to go right away. But Tom said it was too far to go since they were all so tired from their trip.

While they were talking, a man in a new Chevrolet coupe drove into the camp. He said he was looking for workers. But he wouldn't say how much he was going to pay exactly. And he didn't say how many men he'd need.

Floyd got angry. He said if the man didn't know all that, then he shouldn't be hiring men. The contractor called to a man sitting in the car. When he walked over, he had a cartridge belt around his waist. On his brown shirt was a deputy's star.

The contractor pointed to Floyd. "Ever see this fellow before?" the man asked.

"What did he do?" the deputy asked.

"He's talkin' red, causing trouble."

"Seems to me he's the fellow I saw hanging around that used-car lot last week, the one that was busted into. Yep, I'd swear it."

"You got nothing on him," Tom said.

"If you want to join him, open your trap once more. I want all of you out of here by morning. There's plenty of work in Tulare County."

The contractor walked back to the car and got in. The deputy reached out for Floyd. He spun around and socked the deputy, then took off. The deputy staggered, and Tom tripped him. The deputy fell, reaching for his gun. He fired from the ground. Before he could fire again, Casy stepped up and kicked him in the neck. The deputy passed out.

Tom threw the man's gun away. Casy said to him, "You got to get out. He didn't see me kick him. But he saw you trip him."

"I don't want to go," Tom said.

"They'll fingerprint you. You broke parole. They'll send you back."

"Geez, I forgot."

"Go quick," Casy said. "Before he comes to." Tom disappeared in a hurry.

Moments later another sheriff's car came into camp. Four men with rifles piled out. Casy walked over to them. He told them he'd knocked out the deputy. When the deputy came to, he said he wasn't sure it was Casy who hit him. But Casy convinced them, and he was arrested.

Tom returned to the tent. Rose of Sharon was upset. She and Connie had an argument, and he'd walked away. And he hadn't come back. Ma told her she was whining and feeling sorry for herself too much. She put her to work peeling some potatoes.

Later Floyd came by. He said it was best they move out. Once the deputy said to clear out, that meant that some thugs from town would come and burn them out during the night. Al asked him about a government camp he'd heard about.

"Go south on 99 about 12 or 14 miles," Floyd said. "Then turn east to Weedpatch. It's right near there. But I think it's full up."

"Fellow says it's nice there," Al said.

"Sure, it's nice," Floyd said. "Treat you like a man, instead of a dog. No cops there. But it's full up."

Tom told the rest of the family about the danger of the camp being burned out. They

decided to eat quickly and then leave that night. They packed up the truck. Rose of Sharon refused to go without Connie. Al said he'd seen Connie heading south. It looked like he was gone for good. Ma told Rose of Sharon she'd left word at the store where they'd be if Connie returned.

They had to avoid the center of town after they left. A deputy had refused to let them go south through town. Tom drove through side streets and cleared the town. Then he crossed back. At an intersection the sign said "99." He turned south on it.

"Well, we still go where we want, even if we have to crawl for the right," Tom said.

The dim lights fell along the broad black highway ahead.

8 The Government Camp

The moving, questing people were migrants now. They scampered about looking for work. And the highways were streams of people, and the ditch banks were lines of people.

In the West there was panic when the migrants multiplied on the highways. Men of property were terrified for their land. Men who had never been hungry saw the eyes of the hungry.

The men of the towns and the suburban country gathered to defend themselves. They told themselves that they were good and the invaders bad. They said, these darn Okies are dirty and ignorant. They'll steal anything. They've got no sense of property rights.

The local people whipped themselves into a mold of cruelty. Then they formed units and squads armed with clubs, gas, and guns. We own the country. We can't let these Okies get out of hand.

When there was work for a man, ten men fought for it. If that fellow will work for 30 cents, I'll work for 25.

If he'll take 25, I'll do it for 20.

No, me, I'm hungry. I'll work for 15. I'll work for food. I'll work for a little piece of meat.

This was good, for wages went down and prices stayed up. The great owners were glad, and they sent out more handbills to bring more people in.

So, money that might have gone for wages went for guns, for agents and spies, for drilling. On the highways, the people moved like ants and searched for work, for food. And the anger began to grow.

It was late when Tom finally found the government camp. A high wire fence faced the road, and a wide-gated driveway turned in. Tom drove through and stopped at a small house with a light in the window. A watchman stood up from the porch and walked to the truck.

"Say, you got any room for us?" Tom asked.

"Got one camp," the man said. "How many are you?" Tom told him.

"Well I guess we can fix you," the man said. "Drive down the end of that line and turn right. You'll be in Number Four Sanitary Unit."

"What's that?"

"Toilets and showers and wash tubs."

"You got wash tubs—running water?" Ma asked.

"Sure."

"Oh! Praise God," Ma said.

Tom drove down to the sanitary building. Then while the family unloaded, he walked back

64

to the office with the watchman. After the man asked several questions, he told Tom about the camp.

There were five sanitary units. Each one elected a Central Committee representative. This committee made the camp rules and ran things. There was a ladies' committee that helped look after the kids and took care of the sanitary units.

There was one thing that amazed Tom. No cops were allowed in the camp.

"No cop can come in here without a warrant," the man said.

"Well suppose a fellow is just mean or drunk and quarrelsome," Tom said.

"The Central Committee warns him the first two times," the man said. "The third time they kick him out of camp."

"God, I can hardly believe it," Tom said.

"Some nights the boys patrol the fences, to head off trouble," the man said. "Especially dance nights."

"Dance nights!"

"We got the best dances in the country every Saturday night."

"Geez, why aren't there more places like this?" Tom asked.

The watchman looked sad. "You'll have to find that out for yourself. Get some sleep."

"Good night," Tom said. "Ma's going to like this place. She hasn't been treated decent for a long time."

The next morning Tom was awake before the rest of the family. A family a few tents away was having breakfast. The father and son invited Tom to join them. The son told Tom that they'd been working for 12 straight days. He asked him if he wanted to come along and see if he could get some work, too. Tom jumped at the chance.

He ran back toward the Joad tent. Only little Ruthie was awake. Tom quickly told her where he was going. He told her to tell the family when they woke up. Then he ran back and set off down the street with the two men.

Tom introduced himself. The father and son said their names were Timothy and Wilkie Wallace. When they reached the farm, they saw the owner, Mr. Thomas. He told them he had to cut their wages, from 30 cents an hour to 25 cents. He didn't want to do it, and he was angry. He said the Farmer's Association he belonged to had decided the night before to pay only 25 cents. He had to go along.

Mr. Thomas also told them the Association didn't like the government camps. They were planning on causing trouble at the next camp dance on Saturday. Some men would start a fight, maybe even a shooting. Then deputies could go in and clean out the camp.

"Don't ever tell where you heard it," Mr. Thomas said. "But I like you people."

Timothy Wallace said he belonged to the camp's Central Committee. He was grateful for the information. He shook Thomas's hand. "We thank you," he said. "There won't be a fight."

"Will you take 25 cents an hour?" Thomas asked.

"We'll take it—from you," Wilkie said.

The men went to work digging a ditch. And the sun shone hotly down on them in the growing morning.

When Ma woke up, Ruthie told her where Tom had gone. Ma was pleased. She went down to the Sanitary Unit to wash up. While she was there, she met an elderly man. He told her that a ladies' committee would be calling on her soon to explain things about the camp. Ma hurried out and half ran back to the tent.

"Pa," she called. "John, Al, get up and get washed." Startled, sleepy eyes looked out at her. "All of you," Ma cried.

"What's the matter?" Pa demanded.

"There's a committee—a ladies' committee— coming to visit. Get up now and get washed. And while we were sleeping and snoring, Tom went out and got work."

Rose of Sharon crawled out of the tent. Ma looked at her wrinkled, dirty dress, and her frizzled uncombed hair.

"You got to clean up," Ma said briskly. "Go and put on a clean dress. Get the seeds out of your eyes." Ma was excited.

Rose of Sharon said sullenly, "I don't feel good. I wish Connie would come. I don't feel like doing nothing without Connie."

"Rose of Sharon you get upright," Ma said sternly. "You've been mopin' enough. There's a ladies' committee coming. And the family isn't going to be frawny when they get here."

"But I don't feel good. I feel like I'm going to throw up."

"Well, that's okay," Ma said. "Everybody in your condition feels that way. Get it over, then clean up. Wash your legs and put on different shoes. And braid your hair."

Rose of Sharon walked off toward the Sanitary Unit. Soon the men returned along with Ruthie and Winfield. They had all cleaned up. Ma quickly fed them the pone and gravy she'd fixed for breakfast. Then Pa, Uncle John, and Al set off in the truck to look for work.

When Rose of Sharon returned, her hair was dripping and combed. And her skin was bright and pink. She had put on the clean dress and wore the heeled slippers of her wedding. She blushed under Ma's gaze. "You had a bath," Ma said.

Rose of Sharon spoke huskily. "You get in a little stall and you turn handles. And water comes flooding down on you—hot water or cool water, just like you want it."

"I'm going to go myself," Ma said. "Just as soon as I get finished here. You show me how."

"A lady saw my belly," Rose of Sharon went on. "She said they have a nurse here that comes every week. She'll tell me what to do so the baby will be strong. And you know what? Last week there was a baby born, and the whole camp gave a party. They gave clothes and stuff for the baby, even a baby buggy—a wicker one. It wasn't new, but they painted it and it looked new. And they gave the baby a name and had a cake. Oh, Lord!" She finally stopped, breathing heavily.

"Praise God, we come home to our own people," Ma said. "I'm going to have a bath."

Ma and Rose of Sharon cleaned up and straightened out their camp. They cleaned the plates and dishes and put them away. They made the beds and swept up around the tent.

In a little while, the three-member ladies' committee appeared. One of the women said,

"We're going to show you about the sanitary unit first. Then if you want, we'll sign you up in the Ladies' Club and give you your duty. Of course you don't have to join."

"Does it cost much?" Ma asked.

"Doesn't cost nothing but work," the woman said. "And when you're better known, maybe you can be elected to this committee. Well, Mrs. Joad, I guess it's time we told you about how this camp runs."

"This is my girl, Rose of Sharon," Ma said.

"How do," the woman said. "She better come along, too." And they walked off toward the sanitary units.

Pa, Uncle John, and Al returned late in the afternoon. They had driven along beautiful roads. They had gone past orchards where the peaches were beginning to color. They had gone past vineyards with pale and green clusters. And they had gone under lines of walnut trees whose branches spread half across the road. At each entrance gate Al slowed. And at each gate there was a sign: "No help wanted. No trespassing."

When Pa came over to the tent, Ma asked, "Get any work?"

"No," he said, ashamed. "We looked."

"This here is a nice place," Ma said sadly. "We could be happy here awhile."

"If we could get work."

"Yeah. If you could get work."

Uncle John joined them. He squatted down in front of Ma. "We didn't get anywhere. There's no work."

"You didn't look all over," Ma said.

"No, but there's signs out."

"Well, Tom must have gotten work," she said. "He hasn't been back."

"Maybe he went away like Connie or Noah," Uncle John said.

Ma glanced sharply at him. "There are things you know," she said. "Things you're sure of. Tom's got work, and he'll come in this evening. He's a fine boy."

Ma pulled herself together. "Get to the store," she said. "I want beans and sugar, and a piece of frying meat and carrots. And get something— anything—nice for tonight. Tonight, we'll have something nice."

9 Just a Little Pleasure

The migrant people, scuttling for work, scrambling to live, looked always for pleasure. They were hungry for entertainment.

Sometimes there were three men in the evening—playing harmonica, fiddle, and guitar. And the dancing and the singing would start. The fiddle squeaked and the guitar strummed. Harmonica man got red in the face. That Texas boy and the Cherokee girl danced up a storm. The old folks clapped their hands, tapped their feet— and smiled a little.

The migrant people looked humbly for pleasure on the roads.

On Saturday the people in the camp got ready for the big dance that night. The women washed dresses and hung them out to dry. About mid-afternoon child bathing began. Before five, the children were scrubbed and warned about getting dirty again.

By six o'clock the men were back from work, or from looking for work. Then a new wave of bathing started. By seven, the men had on their freshly washed overalls and clean blue shirts.

The girls were ready in their print dresses, stretched and clean.

On the platform, the string band practiced, surrounded by a double wall of children. The people were intent and excited.

Ezra Huston, chairman of the Central Committee, was holding a meeting in his tent. He asked one of the other committee members to go and find Willie Eaton. Willie was chairman of the Entertainment Committee.

When Willie arrived, Huston asked him, "You heard about tonight?"

Willie grinned. "Yeah."

"Did you do anything about it?"

"Well, sir, the ordinary Entertainment Committee is five people. I've added 20 more— all good strong boys. They'll be dancing and keeping their eyes and ears open. The first sign of any talk or argument, they'll close in tight. They'll move the fellow out and nobody will see 'em."

"Tell them not to hurt anybody," Huston said.

"They know. I've got five men out at the gate looking over the folks that come in. They try to spot them before they get started."

"Well, it sounds all right," Huston said. But he was still worried.

Now the dusk was falling. The lights flashed on, and two men inspected the patched wire to the dance floor. From the tents the people streamed toward the platform. They then stood quietly waiting.

Now the families of the guests began to arrive. There were small farmers and migrants from other camps. And as the guests came through the gate, they mentioned the name of the camper who had invited them.

Tom watched the people coming in to the dance. A floodlight shone down on their faces. Willie Eaton said, "Just keep your eyes open. And see if you can pick out the ones."

"Okay," Tom said. Another man came over and stood beside Tom. "I'm Jule," he said. "I'm with you."

Three young men were coming through the gate. They walked close together. The guard at the gate questioned them. They answered and passed through.

Jule walked over to the guard. "Who asked those three fellows there?"

"A fellow named Jackson, Unit Four," the guard said.

Tom and Jule quickly found Jackson and asked him about the three young men. Jackson said he had worked with them recently. But he hadn't invited them to the dance.

Willie said he'd point out the three men to the other members of his committee. They'd all keep an eye out for trouble.

Willie was on the platform. The music was about to start up again. He called out "Choose again for another square, if you can."

The three men reached the middle of the square. One of them said, "I'll dance with this one here."

A blond boy looked up in astonishment. "She's my partner."

"Listen, you no good little—"

Off in the distance, a whistle sounded. The three men were surrounded. Then they were moved off the floor quickly.

Willie called out, "Let's go." And the music started again.

A touring car drove up to the camp entrance. The driver said, "Open up. We hear you got a riot."

The guard stayed still. "We've got no riot. Listen to that music. Who are you?"

"Deputy sheriffs."

"Got a warrant?"

"We don't need a warrant if there's a riot."

"Well, we got no riot here," the guard said.

The car pulled slowly away and parked in a crossroad and waited.

The three troublemakers were brought over to Ezra Huston. Their heads were down. He put a flashlight beam in each sullen face. "What did you want to do it for? he asked. There was no answer. "Who told you to do it?"

"We didn't do anything," one man said. "We were just going to dance."

"No, you weren't," Jule said. "You were gonna sock that kid."

"We're not going to hurt you," Huston said to the men. "Now, who told you to come and bust up our dance? You're our own folks," he added sadly. "You belong with us."

"Well, a fellow's got to eat," one of them said.

"Who sent you? Who paid you to come?"

"We haven't been paid."

"And you're not gonna be," Huston said. "No fight, no pay. Isn't that right?"

"Do what you want," one of the men said. "We're not going to tell anything."

"Okay. Don't tell. But look here. Don't knife your own folks. We're trying to get along, just having fun and keeping order. Don't tear that down."

Huston turned to his men. "All right, boys, put them over the back fence. And don't hurt them. They don't know what they're doing."

Willie, Tom, and the others escorted the men to the back fence. Two of the seated guards stood up and moved over. "Got some fellows going home early," Willie said. The three men climbed over the fence and disappeared into the darkness.

10 Desperate—and on the Run

The spring is beautiful in California. The leaves break out on the trees. And the petals drop from the fruit trees and carpet the earth with pink and white. The centers of the blossoms swell and grow: cherries and apples, peaches and pears.

First the cherries ripen. Cent and a half a pound. Heck, we can't pick them for that. So the birds eat half of each one.

The pears grow yellow and soft. Five dollars a ton. Trees pruned and sprayed, orchards cultivated. Pick the fruit, put it in boxes, load the trucks, deliver them to the cannery. We can't do it. And the fruit falls heavily to the ground.

Then the grapes—we can't make good wine. People can't buy good wine. Rip the grapes from the vines, good grapes, rotten grapes.

The little farmers watched debt creep up on them like the tide. They sprayed the trees and sold no crop. They pruned and grafted and could not pick the crop. This little orchard will be part of a great holding next year. This vineyard will belong to the bank.

Only the great owners can survive, for they own the canneries too. And four pears peeled and cut in half, cooked and canned, still cost 15 cents. They do not spoil. They will last for years.

Carloads of oranges dumped on the ground. The people came for miles to take the fruit. Why would they buy oranges at 20 cents a dozen if they could drive out and pick them up for free? So men with hoses spray kerosene on the oranges. A million people hungry, needing the fruit—and kerosene sprayed over the golden mountains.

And in the eyes of the hungry there is a growing wrath. In the souls of the people the grapes of wrath are filling and growing heavy for the vintage.

A month went by. And the Joad family still could find no work. Only Tom had found work— for five days. For the past two weeks, there had hardly been any food to eat. But everyone was afraid to discuss it. Everyone except Ma.

"We got to do something," she said one night after dinner. "We're down to eatin' fried dough. The money's gone. We got one day more grease and flour, and ten potatoes. And you're all scared to talk about it. Now, you sit here and figure something out."

"We got to go," Pa said. "We didn't want to. We have to go live in one of them Hoovervilles."

"Well if we got to, we got to," Ma said. "First thing is, we got to eat."

"There's hot water here, and toilets—" Pa began.

"Well, we can't eat toilets."

"Fellow says there's cotton coming in up north, near Tulare," Uncle John said. "That's not very far, he says."

"Well, we know there's nothing here," Tom said. "Suppose we pack up and shove north. Then when the cotton is ready, we'll be there. You win, Ma. We'll move on, I guess."

Ma glanced at him. "When?"

"Well, might as well go in the morning."

Ma plunged a dish into a bucket. "We'll go in the morning," she said.

It was still dark when Ma roused her camp. From the tents along the road came the assorted snores of the campers. The family got ready as quickly as possible.

The truck edged slowly out onto the road. Tom drove west until he got to Highway 99. Then he turned north, toward Bakersfield. They hadn't gone very far when they got a flat tire. They stopped by the side of the road. A few minutes later, a brown-faced man stopped on the other side of the road.

The man got out of his car and walked across to the truck. He smiled, and his teeth were very white. He wore a huge wedding ring on his left hand. A little gold football hung on a thin chain across the vest. "Morning," he said pleasantly.

"Morning," Tom said.

"You people looking for work?"

"We sure are, mister."

"Can you pick peaches?"

"We've never done it," Pa said.

"We can do anything," Tom said quickly.

"Well, there's plenty of work for you about 40 miles north. Go north to Pixley, and then turn east. Ask anybody where the Hooper Ranch is. You'll find plenty of work there."

"Thanks a lot, mister," Tom said. "We need work awful bad."

"All right. Get along as soon as you can." He walked across the road. Then he climbed into his car and drove away.

A little before noon, they reached Pixley. They drove through the little town and turned onto a narrower road. The orchards that lined the way made an aisle.

Soon, they could see that the road ahead was blocked with cars. A line of white motorcycles was drawn up along the roadside.

As they got near, a State policeman stopped them. He asked where they were going. Al said they'd heard there was work picking peaches.

"Want to work, do you?" the man asked.

"Darn right," said Tom.

"Okay. Wait a minute." He called ahead and said, "One more. That's six cars ready. Better take this batch through."

"What's the matter?" Tom asked.

"Got a little trouble ahead," the man said. "Don't worry, you'll get through."

The cars drove on, surrounded by motorcycles. Tom looked around. He saw a line of men standing in the ditch beside the road. They were shaking their fists, and their faces were furious.

"These are our own people," Tom said. "I don't like this."

When they were inside the peach camp, the cars stopped. There were 50 little square, flat-roofed boxes, each with a door and a window. Two bookkeepers went from car to car. They assigned the Joads to house number 63. The wages would be five cents a box. No bruised fruit was to be picked.

The Joads found their house. The floor was splashed with grease. In one room stood a rusty tin stove and nothing else. The room smelled of sweat and grease. Rose of Sharon stood beside Ma. "We're gonna live here?"

Ma was silent for a minute. "Why, sure," she said at last. "It won't be so bad once we wash it out and get it mopped."

After the truck was unloaded, the men went to work picking. Even little Ruthie and Winfield went to work. Tom picked three buckets quickly and dumped them in a box. But when he took them in to get checked, they were all rejected. They were bruised. He had to start all over again.

It was a long afternoon. Ma came out and helped pick, too. When the sun went down, they had picked 20 boxes. They had made a dollar.

Ma took a slip of paper with a dollar's worth of credit. Then she walked over to the company store to buy some food. Everything she asked for was more expensive than if she'd bought it in town. But the clerk said he couldn't help it. Those were the prices set by the store owners— Hooper Ranches, Incorporated.

After dinner, Tom decided he'd go outside the gate. He wanted to find out what the trouble had been when they entered the camp. But when he got up to the front gate, a man with a gun stopped him.

"Where are you going?" the man asked.

"Can't I even get out of here?" Tom asked.

"Not tonight," the man said. "Walk back, or I shall whistle for some help and take you."

"Heck, it's nothin' to me," Tom said. And he walked away.

When he'd walked about a hundred yards, he cut across a field. At last he came to a barbed wire fence. He lay on his back and crawled under it. He was about to get up, when a group of men walked by on the edge of the highway. When they were far ahead, he followed them.

He came to a bridge. At the bottom of a ravine, he saw a tent with a lantern burning inside. He climbed down. A man sat on a box in front of the tent.

"Good evening," Tom said.

"Who are you?"

"Well, I'm just going past," Tom said.

"Know anybody here?" the man asked.

A head stuck out of the tent. A voice said, "What's the matter?"

"Casy!" Tom cried. "Casy! For God's sake, what are you doing here?"

"Why, my God, it's Tom Joad! Come on in Tommy, come on in."

"Know him, do you?" the man in front asked.

"Know him? Heck, yes. Known him for years. I come west with him. Come on in Tom."

They went inside the tent. Three other men sat on the ground. Tom shook hands. Then Casy said, "Well, for God's sake, where are your folks? What are you doing here?"

Tom explained to Casy what had happened to the Joads since they'd seen him last. Tom questioned Casy about what had happened to him in jail. Then Tom asked what all the trouble was outside the ranch.

One man said. "This here is a strike."

"Well, five cents isn't much, but a man can eat," Tom said.

"Five cents?" the man cried. "They're paying you five cents?"

"Sure," Tom answered.

A heavy silence fell in the tent. Then Casy said, "Look, Tom. Before we came to work here, they said it was going to be five cents. There was a lot of us. When we got there, they're paying two and a half cents. A fellow can't even eat on that, and if he's got kids— So, we said we won't take it. Then they drove us off. And all the cops in the world came down on us. Now they're paying you five. When they bust this strike, you think they'll pay five?"

"I don't know," Tom said.

"Look," Casy said. "We tried to camp together, and they drove us like pigs. We can't last much longer. Some people haven't eaten for two days. You going back tonight?"

"Yes," Tom said.

"Well, tell the folks in there how it is, Tom. Tell them they're starving us and stabbing themselves in the back. Because as sure as a cow gives milk, it'll drop to two and a half cents as soon as they clear us out."

"I'll tell them," Tom said. "I don't know how. I've never seen so many guys with guns. Don't know if they'll even let a fellow talk."

Just then, the man outside called to them. "What is it?" Casy asked.

"Listen!"

Through the normal sounds of the night, they could hear other sounds. There were faint footsteps from the road, a little swish of brush down the stream.

"You hear it, Tom?" Casy asked.

"I hear it," said Tom. "I think they're guys coming from every which way. We better get out of here."

"Let's go," Casy said.

They hadn't gotten more than 30 feet when a sharp voice called, "There they are!" Two flashlight beams fell on the men. "Stand where you are." The beam fell on Casy. "That's him."

Casy stared blindly at the light. "Listen," he said. "You fellows don't know what you're doing. You're helping to starve kids."

"Shut up, you no good dirty red."

A short heavy man stepped into the light. He carried a white pick handle.

Casy went on. "You don't know what you're doing."

The heavy man swung with the pick handle. The club crashed into the side of Casy's head with a dull crunch of bone. Casy fell sideways out of the light.

"Geez, George, I think you killed him."

"Serve him right. Put the light on him." The flashlight beam found Casy's crushed head.

Tom looked down at the preacher. Then he leaped silently and wrenched the club free. He missed the first time. But the second time his crushing blow found the head. As the man fell down, three more blows smashed his head.

The lights danced about. There were shouts and the sound of running feet crashing through brush. Tom stood over the man. Then a club reached his head, a glancing blow. It felt like an electric shock. Then he ran along the stream, bending low. Suddenly he turned and squirmed up into the brush. And he lay still.

Tom made it back to the house inside the ranch. The rest of the family was asleep. He found a place to lie down, but he could not sleep. His face throbbed, and his cheek bone ached. His broken nose pulsed with pain.

When dawn came, the family slowly stirred. Ma came over to Tom. His face was puffed and blue. The blood was dried on his lips and chin.

"Tom," she said, "what's the matter?"

"I got in a fight. I couldn't help it."

"You in trouble?"

"Yeah," he said. "I can't go out to work. I got to hide." Then Tom explained what had happened to Casy the night before. Ma said she didn't fault him. She wished he hadn't done it, but she couldn't blame him.

The family thought about what to do. They knew they had to leave the ranch. They decided to work all day, make as much money as they could, and then leave that night. They ate breakfast quickly and headed for the fields. Rose of Sharon stayed behind to look after Tom and make sure no one came into the house.

That night the family returned, tired and hungry. They had news, too. The price for picking had dropped to two and a half cents, just as Casy had predicted. And people were saying that the man Tom had hit was dead. No one knew who had done it. But there was talk of finding him and holding a lynching.

The family began loading up the truck. Tom hid on top between two mattresses. As they were finishing, a guard came by, his shotgun across his arm. He asked where they were going. Pa told the man they had been promised some work back down by Weedpatch. The man was suspicious, but he let them go.

Al stopped at the service station and turned over his credit slip for some gas. Then they headed for the front gate. The guard swung the gate open. The truck turned left and moved toward 101, the great north-south highway.

Before long, they passed through all the fruit trees and came upon the cotton fields. Beside a creek, they saw a long line of red boxcars. A sign on the edge of the road said "Cotton Pickers

90

Wanted." A little past the sign, Tom called down for Al to stop the truck.

Tom suggested that the family look for work picking cotton. They could live in the boxcars with the other workers. While they did, he would hide out by the nearby creek. At night, someone could bring him some food to eat. Then when his face healed, he could join the rest of the family.

"It seems like good sense to me," Pa said.

"It is good sense," Tom insisted. "As soon as my face is better, I'll go picking, too."

Tom went back up top and took a blanket.

"Take care," Ma begged. "You take care."

"Sure, I will," Tom said and disappeared into the bushes beside the stream.

Al drove slowly back to the line of boxcars. The truck lights showed the catwalks up to the wide car doors. The doors were dark. No one moved in the night. Al shut off his lights.

"Dear Jesus, I hope it's all right," Ma said.

11 A Sad Good-bye

Cotton Pickers Wanted.
I aim to pick some cotton.
Got a bag?
Well, no.
Cost you a dollar, the bag. Take it out of your first 150. Eighty cents first time over the field. Ninety cents second time over.

Now the bag is heavy, boost it along. Set your hips and tow it along, like a work horse. Good crop here. Sack's full now. Take it to the scales. Argue. Scale man says you got rocks to make weight. How about him? His scales are fixed. Sometimes he's right, you got rocks in the sack. Sometimes you're right, the scales are crooked. Sometimes both are right.

Come night, all tired. Good pickin' though. Got three dollars, me, the woman, and the kids. Wish it would last. It's not much money, God knows. But I wish it would last.

Side-meat tonight, by God. We got money for side-meat. The woman will make some biscuits, too, if she's not too tired.

The Joads had been lucky. They got in early enough to have a place in the boxcars. Soon, the tents of the late-comers filled up the area.

The cars were water-tight and draftless. Each car was big enough for two families to share. The Joads had one end of a car. Ma hung a tarpaulin across the middle for privacy.

Every day they went into the fields and picked the cotton. And every night they had meat, and milk for Rose of Sharon. On a Saturday they drove into town. They bought a tin stove and some new clothes for all of them.

One evening, Winfield told Ma that Ruthie had gotten into a fight with some other kids. When a big girl beat her up, Ruthie said she had a big brother who would kill her. She said her brother had killed two men and was hiding.

When Pa returned, Ma told him what happened. "I'm going out to find Tom and tell him to be careful," she said. "I'll take him some dinner."

Ma walked passed all the boxcars and the tents. Then she stepped into the willows beside the stream. She moved off the trail and listened to make sure she wasn't being followed. She waited, and then walked on.

After awhile she came to the place where Tom said he'd be hiding. She heard someone step among the leaves to her left, and she grew tense. She saw a figure creep into the open. "Tom," she called softly. The figure stood still. "Tom, oh Tom," she called again.

"Is that you, Ma?"

"Right over here," she said and stood up. "I got to see you, Tom. I got to talk to you."

"Come along," he said. "Quiet now."

When they were deep in the brush, Tom leaned over and pulled a mat of vines aside. "You got to crawl in," Tom said.

Ma went into the cave on her hands and knees. It was completely dark. "Where are you, Ma?" Tom said.

"Here, right here. Talk soft, Tom."

"Don't worry. I've been living like a rabbit for some time."

She heard him unwrap his tin plate.

"Pork chops and fried potatoes," she said.

"God Almighty, and still warm."

Ma said uneasily, "Tom, Ruthie told about you." She heard him gulp.

"What for?"

"Well, it wasn't her fault." Ma told him about Ruthie's fight with the other girl.

"The kids will tell it all around, and then their folks will hear," Ma said. "Pretty soon, they're liable to get men out to look. Tom, you got to go away."

"That's what I said right along. I was always scared somebody would find me out."

"I know," Ma said. "But I wanted you near. I was scared for you. I haven't seen you. I can't see you now. How's your face?"

"Getting well quick."

She crawled close to his voice. She touched his face all over. "I want to remember, even if it's only my fingers that remember. You got to go away, Tom. We've been doing pretty good," Ma said. "Hold out your hand. I got seven dollars here."

"I'm not going to take your money."

"You take this money. You got no right to cause me pain."

"You're not playing fair," he said.

"I thought maybe you could go to a big city like Los Angeles. They would never look for you there."

"Look, Ma, I've been doing a lot of thinking," he said. "I've been thinking about Casy. How he said one time he went out in the wilderness to find his own soul. But he found that he didn't have a soul that was his. Said he found he just has a little piece of a great big soul. He said the wilderness wasn't any good because his little piece of soul wasn't with the rest."

"He was a good man," Ma said.

"I've been thinking how it was in that government camp," he said. "How our folks took care of themselves. I've been wondering why we can't do that all over. All work together for our own thing—all farm our own land."

"What are you going to do?" Ma asked.

"What Casy did."

"But they killed him."

"Yeah," Tom said. "He didn't duck fast enough. But he wasn't doing anything against the law."

"But how am I going to know about you?" she asked. "They might hurt you. How am I going to know?"

"Well, maybe like Casy says, a fellow hasn't got a soul of his own. So then—"

"Then what, Tom?"

"Then it doesn't matter. Then I'll be around in the dark. I'll be everywhere. Wherever there's a fight so hungry people can eat, I'll be there. Wherever there's a cop beating up a guy, I'll be there. I'll be in the way guys yell when they're mad. I'll be in the way kids laugh when they're hungry and they know supper is ready. And when our folks eat the stuff they raise, and live in the houses they build—why, I'll be there. See?"

"I don't understand," Ma said.

"Me neither," Tom said. "It's just stuff I've been thinking about. You got to go back, Ma."

"You take the money, then."

He was silent for a moment. "All right."

"And, Tom, later, when it's blown over, you'll come back. You'll find us?"

"Sure," he said. "Now you better go. Here, give me your hand." He guided her to the entrance and then followed her out. "Good-bye."

"Good-bye," she said. Her eyes were wet and burning. But she did not cry.

That night when Al returned to the boxcar, he had an announcement. He and Aggie Wainwright were going to get married. Aggie was the daughter of the family that was sharing the boxcar with the Joads. They had been going out every night for days, and had fallen in love.

The two families were happy. They didn't have a cake, but Ma made some coffee and cooked some pancakes to celebrate.

The next morning, everyone went out into the fields to pick the cotton. Rose of Sharon insisted on going, too, even though Ma said she was too far along. By late morning the picking was all done. And then the rain began.

By the time they got back to the boxcar, they were all soaked. And Rose of Sharon was shivering from the cold. Ma brought her blankets, and the men kept the fire going in the stove.

The evening came early. In the boxcars the families huddled together, listening to the pouring water on the roofs.

12 Fighting for Survival

The rain began with gusty showers. Then it settled into a steady beat. At first the dry earth sucked the moisture down. Then puddles formed in the fields. At last the mountains were full, and the hillsides spilled into the streams. It sent them roaring down the canyons into the valleys.

In the migrant camps, the tents and old cars stood. The water fouled the cars' motors, and the little gray tents stood in lakes. At last the people had to move. But the cars wouldn't start. So the people waded away. They carried their children and their blankets with them. And if a barn stood on high ground, it was filled with people, shivering and hopeless.

Slowly, the greatest terror of all came along. There won't be any work for three months. In the barns, the people sat huddled together as the terror came over them. The children cried with hunger, and there was no food. Then the sickness came, pneumonia and measles. And the rain fell steadily.

In the wet hay of leaking barns, babies were born to women who panted with pneumonia. And old people curled up in corners and died that way. At night desperate men walked boldly to hen roosts and carried off the squawking chickens. If they were shot at, they did not run. They just splashed sullenly in the mud. And if they were hit, they sank tiredly in the mud.

The women watched the men, watched to see whether the break had come at last. When the men gathered together, the fear left their faces and anger took its place. The women sighed with relief. They knew the break would never come as long as fear could turn to wrath.

On the third day, the sound of the stream could be heard above the drumming rain. Pa and Uncle John stood in the open door. They looked out on the rising stream.

"How does it look to you, John?" Pa asked. "It seems to me that if that creek comes up, it'll flood us."

"Yeah," he said. "It might."

"If we all got our shovels and put up a bank, we could keep the water out," Pa said.

"Yeah," Uncle John said. "Suppose those other fellows don't want to. Maybe they want to move some place else."

"But these cars are dry," Pa said. "Couldn't find any place as dry as this. I think we ought to go talk to the other fellows. If they don't want to dig, then we'll have to go." They hunched their shoulders and ran over to the next car.

Rose of Sharon was down with a heavy cold. Her face was flushed and her eyes were shining with fever. Ma kept her covered and gave her hot milk.

Suddenly, a sharp cry came from the mattresses where Rose of Sharon lay. The girl was holding her breath and her eyes were filled with terror.

Ma quickly called Mrs. Wainwright over. They talked with Rose of Sharon. They decided that the time had come for the baby. They tried to make her as comfortable as possible. Every few moments, the girl stiffened with pain.

"Easy," Ma said. "It's going to be all right." The two older women helped her to her feet so she could walk around the boxcar.

When Pa returned, Ma said, "Rose of Sharon's time has come."

"Then we couldn't go if we wanted to."

"No."

"Then we've got to build that bank."

Pa quickly went outside in the rain. He gathered some men around, and they began building the bank.

The evening came, and the work went on. The pains for Rose of Sharon were now 20 minutes apart. The girl screamed fiercely. The neighbor women took turns looking after her. For a long time the screams continued from the car. And at last they stopped.

The men had built the bank up quite high. But then a great cottonwood tree toppled into the stream. The rushing water carried the tree right into the bank. It tore through it, and the water came rushing down.

The men broke and ran. The current worked smoothly into the flat, under the boxcars, under the automobiles. When the dike swept, Al turned and ran for the truck. He tried and tried, but it wouldn't start.

Pa and Uncle John made it back to the boxcar. Ma sat on the mattress beside Rose of Sharon.

"How is she?" Pa asked.

"All right, I think. She's sleeping."

Mrs. Wainwright came over and pulled Pa toward the corner. She held a lantern over a spread out newspaper. On it lay a stillborn baby.

"Never breathed," Mrs. Wainwright said. "Never was alive."

"Think she's going to be all right?" Pa asked.

"I don't know." Ma answered.

"Well, could we have done something else?"

"No," Ma said. "There was only one thing to do. And we did it."

Pa, Al, and Uncle John sat in the doorway and watched the steely dawn come. The rain had stopped. But the sky was deep and solid with color. And the water continued to rise.

"Think it will come inside the car?" Al asked.

"Can't tell. There's a lot of water to come down from the hills yet. And it might start to rain again."

Al had an idea. He knew the truck wouldn't be ready to use for some time. So he wanted to take the sides down and build a platform inside the car. Then they could put all the stuff on the platform and keep things dry if the boxcar flooded.

Pa looked out at the water. "It sure keeps climbing," he said. "I guess we better do that."

Al told Ma what they were going to do. "We got to get out of here," she said.

Rose of Sharon woke up. "How do you feel?" Ma asked.

"Tired," she answered. "Very tired." The girl's eyes questioned Ma, and Ma tried to avoid the question. "Is—it—all right?" she asked.

Ma kneeled down on the mattress. "We did everything we knew," she said.

Rose of Sharon pushed herself up. "Ma!"

"You couldn't help it," she said.

Pa came back from buying some things for breakfast. He used up the last of their money. "Now what are we going to do?" Ma asked.

The family huddled on the platforms. The water was six inches deep in the car. During the day and night, the men slept side by side. And Ma lay close to Rose of Sharon.

When the morning came Rose of Sharon whispered to Ma. She nodded her head. "We're getting out of here," she said angrily. "We're getting to higher ground. I'm taking Rose of Sharon and the little ones. You coming or not?"

"We can't," Pa said weakly.

"It's not raining now, and we're going."

"All right, we'll go," Pa said.

"Ma, I'm not going," Al said.

"Why not?"

"Well, Aggie and me—"

Ma smiled. "Of course," she said. "You stay here, Al. When the water stops, we'll come back. Come on Rose of Sharon, we're going to a dry place."

They left the boxcar. They carried Ruthie and Winfield on their backs. Ma and Pa each held one of Rose of Sharon's hands as they walked slowly through the moving water.

The rain had started to fall again. They walked along the road and through the flooded fields. Then far off the road, on a slight rolling hill, a rain-blackened barn stood. "Look, there," Ma said. "Let's go in there until the rain stops."

They reached the barn. When they settled down on the hay, Winfield cried out, "Look."

Ma looked. There were two figures in the gloom. A man was laying on his back. And a boy was sitting beside him. The boy got up and slowly came over to them. "You own this place?" he said.

"No," Ma said. "Just came in out of the rain. We got a sick girl. You got a dry blanket we can use?"

The boy went back and got a dirty comforter and handed it to Ma.

"Thank you," Ma said. "What's the matter with that fellow?"

"First he was sick," the boy said. "Now he's starving. He hasn't eaten for six days."

"Your pa?" Ma asked.

"Yeah," the boy said. "He gave me the food. Now he's too weak. He can't move."

"Be easy," Ma said. "Let me get the wet clothes off my girl. We'll figure something out."

The boy went away while Ma undressed Rose of Sharon and covered her with the blanket. The boy came back.

"Last night, I busted a window and stole some bread," he said. "But he threw it all up. He's got to have soup or milk. You folks got money to get milk?"

"Hush," Ma said. "Don't worry. We'll figure something out."

"He's dying!" the boy cried.

"Hush," Ma said. She looked at Rose of Sharon, huddled in the comforter. The two women looked deep into each other. "He needs milk," Ma said.

Rose of Sharon's breath came short and gasping. "Yes," the girl said. "I understand."

Ma said quietly, "I knew you would."

Rose of Sharon asked the others to go outside. She got up and walked over to the corner. She stood looking down at the wasted face, into the wide frightened eyes.

She lay down beside him. Her lips came together and smiled mysteriously.